The Legend of
❋ the Poinsettia ❋

retold and illustrated by
Tomie dePaola

Penguin Putnam Books for Young Readers

To Chris O'Brien, who knows
that the beauty of the gift is in the giving.

Copyright © 1994 by Tomie dePaola.
All rights reserved. This book, or parts thereof, may not be reproduced in any form without permission in writing
from the publisher. A PaperStar Book, published in 1997 by Penguin Putnam Books for Young Readers,
345 Hudson Street, New York, NY 10014. PaperStar is a registered trademark of The Putnam Berkley Group, Inc.
The PaperStar logo is a trademark of The Putnam Berkley Group, Inc. Originally published in 1994 by G. P. Putnam's Sons.
Published simultaneously in Canada. Printed in Hong Kong
Library of Congress Cataloging-in-Publication Data
DePaola, Tomie. The legend of the poinsettia / Tomie dePaola.   p.   cm.
Summary: When Lucida is unable to finish her gift for the Baby Jesus in time for the Christmas
procession, a miracle enables her to offer the beautiful flower we now call the poinsettia.
[1. Folklore—Mexico. 2. Poinsettias—Folklore.]   I. Title. PZ8.1.D43Lf 1993 398.24'2—dc20 [E] 92-20459 CIP AC
ISBN 0-698-11567-8 (English)
0-698-11568-6 (Spanish)
5   7   9   10   8   6

Lucida lived in a small village
high up in the mountains of Mexico
with her mama, her papa,
and her younger brother and sister, Paco and Lupe.
Papa worked in the fields with their burro, Pepito.
Every evening Lucida fed Pepito, gave him fresh water,
and filled his stall with clean straw.

At home Lucida helped Mama
clean their *casita*—their little house—
and pat out the tortillas for their meals.

She took care of Paco and Lupe, and each evening
they went to the shrine of the Virgin of Guadalupe
near the front gate to see if fresh candles were needed.

But every day was not work.
On Sundays the family went to San Gabriel
in the square where Padre Alvarez said the Mass.
And all through the year there were fiestas
and holy days, which always began with a procession
that wound through the village and ended in San Gabriel.

One day, close to Christmas—*la Navidad*—
Padre Alvarez came to their casita.
"Ah, Señora Martinez, *buenos días*—good day,"
Padre Alvarez said. "I am here to ask you about the blanket
which covers the figure of the Baby Jesus
in the Christmas procession.

We have used the same one for so many years
that it is almost worn out.
Because your weaving is so fine, I have come to ask
if you would make a new one."
"*Mi padre*," Lucida's mother said, "I would be honored.
And Lucida will help me."

On Saturday Lucida and Mama went to the market
to buy the wool for the blanket. They chose
the finest yarn they could find.

At home Lucida helped Mama dye the wool
the colors of the rainbow.
"Those colors will shine throughout the church,"
Papa said, as he watched Lucida and Mama
string the yarn on the loom.

As Christmas drew closer,
everyone in the village was busy.
All the mamas were making gifts to place
at the manger of the Baby Jesus in the church.
The papas worked together putting up
the manger scene in San Gabriel.

Lucida and the other children went to the church
for singing practice for the Christmas Eve procession,
when everyone would walk to San Gabriel,
singing and carrying candles.
Once inside, Padre Alvarez would lay
the figure of the Baby Jesus in the manger,
and the villagers would go up
and place their gifts around it.
"Our gift will be the blanket for the Baby Jesus,"
Lucida told her friends. "I am helping Mama weave it."

One afternoon a few days before Christmas Eve,
Lucida and the children were singing in the church
when Señora Gomez came hurrying in.
"Lucida, you must come home. Your mama is sick
and your papa has taken her down to the town
to see the doctor. You must take care of your
brother and sister until your papa returns tonight."
Lucida was frightened. Mama had never been sick before.

When she got home, Paco and Lupe were crying.
They were frightened, too. Lucida tried to comfort them.
She made some food and sat down to wait for Papa.

That evening Papa came in looking tired and worried.
He drew Lucida close and said, "Lucida, *mi niña*,
your mama is ill. Your aunt—Tía Carmen—
will take care of Mama until she is well,
but I must go back and stay with Mama
until I can bring her home.
But it won't be until after Christmas.
Señora Gomez will take care of you and Paco and Lupe
while I am gone. She will come for you tomorrow."

The next afternoon Lucida overheard two women talking.
"Lucida's mama is ill. She won't be able to finish
the blanket for the procession. Isn't it a shame?"
"*Sí*," the other woman said. "We are all so disappointed.
Padre Alvarez will have to use the old worn-out one."

When Lucida went home to feed Pepito
and get clothes for Paco, Lupe, and herself,
she looked at the unfinished blanket on the loom.

Perhaps I can finish it, she thought.
But when she sat down and tried to weave,
the yarn got tangled. The more she tried
to untangle it, the worse it got. It was no use.
She could never finish it by herself.

She took the unfinished blanket to Señora Gomez.
"Oh, Lucida, it is so tangled. There isn't time
for me to fix it," Señora Gomez told her.
"Tomorrow is Christmas Eve."
Lucida started to cry.
It was her fault the blanket was ruined.

Her family wouldn't have a gift
to place at the manger of the Baby Jesus.
"Don't worry, Lucida. We will all go
to the procession together."
Lucida didn't say anything, but in her heart
she felt that she had ruined Christmas.

"Come, Paco; come, Lupe. It is time to go to the procession,"
Señora Gomez called on Christmas Eve. "Where is Lucida?"
She was nowhere to be found. Lucida was hiding.

From the shadows, Lucida watched everyone gather
for the procession. The candles were lit, the singing began,
and the villagers walked to San Gabriel,
carrying gifts to place at the manger.
Lucida walked along in the darkness
and watched the procession go into the church,
followed by Padre Alvarez carrying the Baby Jesus.

"Little girl, are you Lucida?" An old woman
stood in the shadows nearby.
"*Sí*," Lucida answered, wondering who she was.
"I have a message for you. Your mama is going to be fine,
and your papa will bring her home soon.
So you don't have to worry.
Go now into the church and celebrate Christmas
with the others. Paco and Lupe are waiting for you."

"I can't," Lucida told her. "I don't have a gift
for the Baby Jesus.
Mama and I were weaving a beautiful blanket,
but I couldn't finish it.
I tried, but I only tangled it all up."
"Ah, Lucida, any gift is beautiful because it is given,"
the old woman told her. "Whatever you give, the Baby Jesus
will love, because it comes from you."
"But what can I give now?" Lucida said, looking around.

A patch of tall green weeds grew in a tangle nearby.
Lucida rushed over and picked an armful.
"Do you think these will be all right?" Lucida turned
to ask the old woman, but she was gone.

Lucida walked into the church. It was blazing
with candlelight, and the children were singing
as she walked quietly down the aisle
with a bundle of green weeds in her arms.

"What is Lucida carrying?" a woman whispered.
"Why is she bringing weeds into the church?"
another one murmured.
Lucida reached the manger scene. She placed the green weeds around the stable. Then she lowered her head and prayed.

A hush fell over the church. Voices began to whisper.
"Look! Look at the weeds!"
Lucida opened her eyes and looked up.

Each weed was tipped with a flaming red star.
The manger glowed and shimmered
as if lit by a hundred candles.

When everyone went outside after the Mass,
all the clumps of tall green weeds
throughout the town were shining with red stars.
Lucida's simple gift had indeed become beautiful.

And every Christmas to this day, the red stars shine
on top of green branches in Mexico. The people
call the plants *la Flor de Nochebuena*—
the Flower of the Holy Night—the poinsettia.

Author's Note

When I first heard the Mexican legend of the poinsettia, about a little girl who offers weeds to the Christ Child as her gift for Christmas, I was touched by it as only Christmas can touch me. I knew that one day I wanted to create the story in pictures for children.

This lovely Mexican wildflower is known by many names in Mexico: *flor de fuego* (fire flower), *flor de Navidad* (Christmas flower), and *flor de la Nochebuena* (flower of the Holy Night), the name I have used in my story.

The poinsettia found its way to the United States through Dr. Joel Roberts Poinsett, who served as our nation's minister to Mexico from 1825 to 1830. He was fascinated with its beauty and called the plant "painted leaves," because the part often thought of as the flower actually consists of leaves surrounding a smaller flower portion. He took cuttings home with him to South Carolina when he returned from Mexico in 1830.

The Christmas plant, which we call poinsettia after Dr. Poinsett, found its way into our own Christmas traditions, and nothing seems to say "Merry Christmas" better than a beautiful red and green poinsettia.

TdeP